NBA CHAMPIONSHIPS:

↓

57, 1959, 1960, 1961, 1962, 1963, 1964, 1965, 1966, 1968, 1969, 1974, 1976, 1981, 1984, 1986, 2008

↓

ALL-TIME LEADING SCORER:

↓

JOHN HAVLICEK (1962–78):

↓

26,395 POINTS

THE NBA:
A HISTORY
OF HOOPS

BOSTON
CELTICS

BY JIM WHITING

CREATIVE EDUCATION CREATIVE PAPERBACKS

Published by Creative Education
and Creative Paperbacks

P.O. Box 227, Mankato, Minnesota 56002

Creative Education and Creative Paperbacks
are imprints of The Creative Company

www.thecreativecompany.us

Design and production by Blue Design
Printed in the United States of America

Photographs by Corbis (Bettmann), Getty
Images (ABC Photo Archives/Contributor,
Brian Babineau/NBAE, Steve Babineau/NBAE,
Al Bello/Getty Images Sport, Andrew D.
Bernstein/NBAE, Bettmann, John Biever/Sports
Illustrated, Kevin C. Cox/Getty Images Sport,
Steve Dunwell, Focus on Sport, Walter Iooss
Jr./NBAE, Walter Iooss Jr./Sports Illustrated,
Matthew J. Lee/The Boston Globe, Bob Levey/
Getty Images Sport, Richard Meek/Sports
Illustrated, Maddie Meyer/Getty Images Sport,
Manny Millan/Sports Illustrated, NBAP/NBAE,
Christian Petersen, Dick Raphael/NBAE)

Library of Congress Cataloging-in-Publication Data

Names: Whiting, Jim, 1943- author.

Title: Boston Celtics / Jim Whiting.

Series: The NBA: A History of Hoops.

Includes bibliographical references and index.

Summary: This high-interest title summarizes
the history of the Boston Celtics professional
basketball team, highlighting memorable events
and noteworthy players such as Bill Russell.

Identifiers: LCCN 2016046221 / ISBN 978-1-60818-
836-9 (hardcover) / ISBN 978-1-62832-439-6
(pbk) / ISBN 978-1-56660-884-8 (eBook)

Subjects: LCSH: 1. Boston Celtics (Basketball
team)—History—Juvenile literature.
2. Boston Celtics (Basketball team)—
Biography—Juvenile literature.

Classification: LCC GV885.52.B67 W558 2017 /
DDC 796.323/640974461—dc23

CCSS: RI.4.1, 2, 3, 4; RI.5.1, 2, 4; RI.6.1, 2,
3; RF.4.3, 4; RF.5.3, 4; RH. 6-8. 4, 5, 7

First Edition HC 9 8 7 6 5 4 3 2 1
First Edition PBK 9 8 7 6 5 4 3 2 1

CONTENTS

LEGENDS OF THE HARDWOOD

BOSTON, Massachusetts, is known as the birthplace of the American Revolution.

LAYING THE FOUNDATION

Only a few seconds remained in the second overtime of Game 7 of the 1957 National Basketball Association (NBA) Finals. The Celtics had led for most of the game. The St. Louis Hawks battled back.

The Celtics fought a close matchup with the Hawks to win their first NBA title in 1957.

They sank key baskets at the end of regulation and the first overtime to stay alive. Now the score was tied 123–123. Burly Boston forward Jim Loscutoff was fouled as he squared up to take a shot. Loscutoff wasn't a very good free-throw shooter. "I don't remember much about those foul shots," he said years later. "I think my hands were shaking, but I made them." St. Louis had one final chance. Hawks star Bob Pettit grabbed a long pass and put up a shot. It bounced off the rim. Another St. Louis player tipped it in. But not before the buzzer sounded. The Celtics won their first NBA championship!

The Celtics' history dates back to 1946. At that time, professional hockey and college basketball were the country's most popular sports. Fans packed the big-city arenas where the games were played. Arena owners wanted another sport to attract fans on nights

12

GOOD ADVICE

CHUCK CONNORS, FORWARD, 6-FOOT-5, 1946–48

Chuck Connors wasn't much of a basketball player. He averaged just 4.5 points a game. His chief claim to fame was as the first player to shatter a backboard. That happened while he was practicing dunks before a game in 1946. He joked that public speaking to drum up interest for the team was his greatest contribution. Boston Red Sox legend Ted Williams was in the audience one time. "He said to me, 'Kid, I don't know what kind of basketball player you are, but you ought to give it up and be an actor,'" Connors recalled. He took the advice. He starred in *The Rifleman*, a popular television show, from 1958 to 1963.

without hockey and college games. Walter Brown, the owner of Boston Garden, called a meeting of those owners. They formed the Basketball Association of America (BAA). The new league had 10 other teams besides Boston. Brown needed a nickname for his team. Fan suggestions included Olympians, Whirlwinds, and Unicorns. Someone even suggested Yankees—the nickname of Boston's baseball rivals in New York City! Brown chose Celtics. Historically, the Celts were peoples who spread from Central Europe to the British Isles in ancient times. Celtic culture especially took hold in Ireland, the homeland of many Bostonians. There had also been a traveling basketball team called the Celtics. They played from 1914 to 1939. One year, that team won 193 games while losing just 11.

T he new team got off to a slow start. It had losing records the first three seasons. But the Celtics made the playoffs after

Coach **RED AUERBACH** led Boston to 9 league championships in 10 years.

the 1947–48 season. They lost to the Chicago Stags in the first round,
two games to one. The BAA merged with the National Basketball League
to form the NBA before the 1949–50 season. Boston finished last in the
new league's Eastern Division.

T he arrival of forward "Easy Ed" Macauley and point
guard Bob Cousy in 1950 helped turn things around. Macauley averaged
20 points a game. Cousy provided floor leadership and flashy street
moves. He was especially known for his behind-the-back dribble. The
team also added Arnold "Red" Auerbach as coach. Under Auerbach's
demanding guidance, the Celtics went 39–30 to record their first winning
season. But they lost in the Eastern Division semifinals. The next season,
Boston added high-scoring guard Bill Sharman. In 1954, Boston drafted
guard/forward Frank Ramsey. When Auerbach needed scoring punch,
he made Ramsey the first player off the bench. This pioneered the "sixth

"EASY ED" MACAULEY was known for his hook shot and passing skills.

man" concept, in which the player had to produce immediately after sitting for so long. A teammate said, "One time … Frank came into the game and he got to the free throw line so quickly that he was too 'cold' to take his shot. He had to warm up before shooting."

During this time, Boston consistently made the playoffs but could never get past the divisional finals. There was a simple reason. The Celtics couldn't stop other teams from scoring. Opponents averaged 101.5 points against them per game in 1954–55. It was the worst mark in the NBA. That situation was about to change.

LEGENDS OF THE HARDWOOD

COOZ TO THE RESCUE

GAME 2, EASTERN DIVISION SEMIFINALS, BOSTON VS. SYRACUSE, MARCH 21, 1953

Playing with an injured leg, Bob Cousy scored 25 points at the end of regulation time. Then he netted six more points in the first overtime. He scored all four of his team's points in a low-scoring second overtime, which ended with another tie. Cousy's last-second, 25-foot shot kept the teams still tied in the third overtime. Boston broke away to win 111–105 in the fourth overtime as Cousy scored 9 of Boston's 12 points. He finished with 50 points. He sank 30 of 32 free throws, an NBA playoffs record for most in a game. "I could go all night on what that kid did," said coach Red Auerbach.

18

THE DYNASTY BEGINS

Boston's 1956 NBA Draft choices and related roster moves became legendary. It was the greatest single-season pickup of talent in NBA history. The Celtics claimed star forward Tommy Heinsohn

Star forward **TOMMY HEINSOHN** earned NBA Rookie of the Year honors in 1957.

Superb ball-snatcher **BILL RUSSELL** nabbed the MVP award five times.

as a territorial pick. He had played his college ball at Holy Cross in nearby Worcester. Then team officials traded Macauley and another player to St. Louis for shot-blocking center Bill Russell. As the official Celtics website notes, "Russell ... turned Boston into an unstoppable force." In the second round, Boston added Russell's college teammate, guard K. C. Jones. Military service kept Jones from joining the team for two years.

Boston cruised to a 44–28 record in Russell's first year. The Celtics swept Syracuse in the Eastern Division finals. Then they claimed their first NBA title by defeating St. Louis when Loscutoff sank his two free throws. The two teams met in the Finals again the following year. Russell hurt his ankle in Game 3. Once again, the series went to a deciding Game 7. This time, Pettit led his team to

The **BOSTON CELTICS** teams of the late 1950s and '60s dominated the NBA.

a 110–109 victory, scoring 19 of the Hawks' final 21 points.

Starting in 1958–59, the Celtics went on a tear. K. C. Jones returned from the military, and second-year forward Sam Jones came into his own. Boston averaged 58 wins a season for 8 years. (It won four out of every five games played.) In 1961–62, the Celtics became the first team to notch 60 victories. They did even better in 1964–65, winning 62 games. The Celtics were NBA champions all eight years. Only twice did the Finals go to a seventh game. As older players such as Cousy and Sharman

LEGENDS OF THE HARDWOOD

"RED" CREATES GREEN PRIDE

When he was in high school, Arnold "Red" Auerbach thought he wanted to become a physical education teacher. Instead, he became one of the best, most-decorated coaches in NBA history. He was a fiery coach who demanded the best from his players. He was especially famous for lighting a victory cigar every time he thought the Celtics had notched another win. To honor him, the NBA awards the Red Auerbach Trophy to the league's best coach every year. "This was a simple no-brainer to name this trophy after Red and for all that he has done for the game of basketball," said NBA commissioner David Stern.

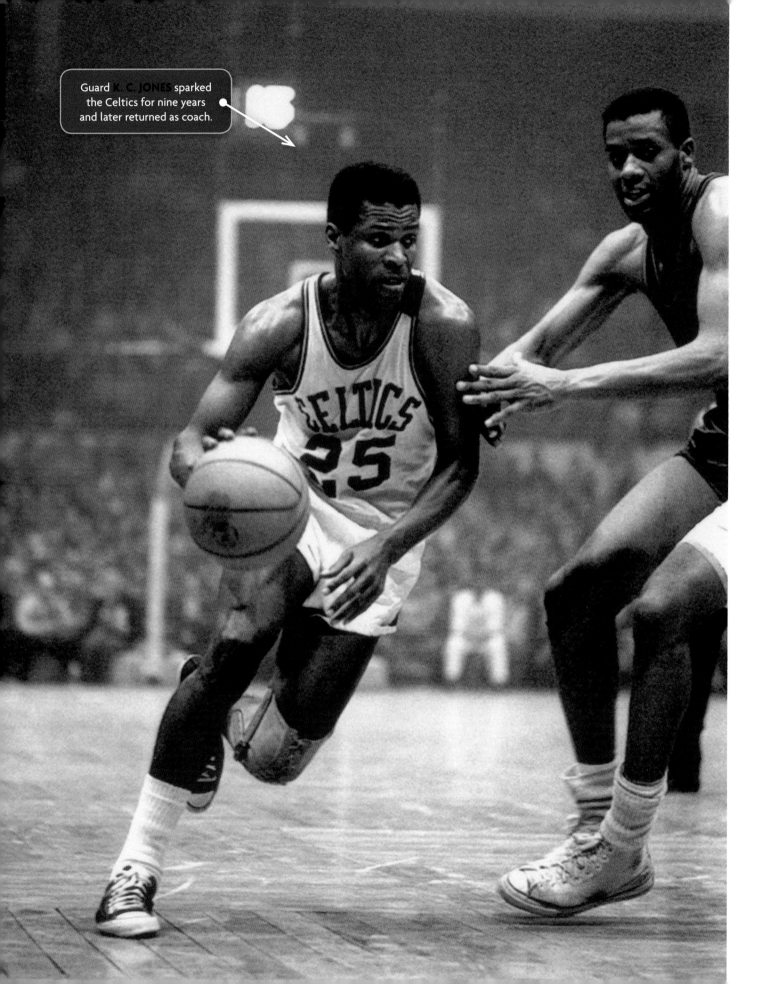

Guard **K. C. JONES** sparked the Celtics for nine years and later returned as coach.

Tireless forward and guard
JOHN HAVLICEK was Boston's
all-time leading scorer.

retired, others took their places. These included forwards Thomas
"Satch" Sanders and John Havlicek, who assumed Ramsey's sixth-man
role. Highlights from this era included Russell's on-court duels with Wilt
Chamberlain of the Philadelphia (later San Francisco) Warriors. Many
people think their personal rivalry is the greatest in NBA history. After
the Celtics notched their eighth title in a row in 1966, Auerbach stepped
down. Russell replaced him as player/coach.

Then a new "Beast of the East" arose. Chamberlain, now playing for
the Philadelphia 76ers, headed a cast that overwhelmed opponents en
route to a 68–13 record. Boston had a respectable 60–21 mark but fell to
the 76ers in the divisional finals.

KEEPING THE
DREAM ALIVE

hough the Celtics were aging,
Russell capably prepared his team for playoff action.
The following year, the Celtics turned the tables on
Philadelphia. In Game 7 of the Eastern Division finals,

Big and quick, **JOHN HAVLICEK** was known for wearing down opponents.

FANTASTIC FINISH

GAME 5, NBA FINALS, BOSTON VS. PHOENIX, JUNE 4, 1976

With the 1976 Finals series tied, Game 5 was critical. At the end of the second overtime, Celtics forward John Havlicek banked in a 15-footer. But as fans poured onto the floor, the referees put two seconds back on the clock. Suns guard Paul Westphal intentionally called a timeout. Because the Suns had used all their timeouts, they were called for a technical foul. Westphal knew that meant the Suns would get the ball at halfcourt. Suns forward Gar Heard took the inbound pass near the top of the key. Then he whirled and drained the ball with a defender in his face to tie the score! It became known as "the shot heard 'round the world." Boston surged to a six-point lead late in the third overtime. It held on for a dramatic 128–126 victory. Two days later, Boston claimed the championship.

LEGENDS OF THE HARDWOOD

Russell took over the final minute. He sank a free throw, blocked a shot, hauled down a rebound, and made an assist. Boston won, 100–96. Boston ranked fourth in the division in 1968–69, but Russell rallied the team. The Celtics beat the Los Angeles Lakers in the NBA Finals, four games to three. It was his 11th championship ring. No one else has won as many. "There are two types of superstars," said Russell's teammate Don Nelson. "One makes himself look good at the expense of the other guys on the floor. But there's another type who makes the players around him look better than they are, and that's the type Russell was."

Both Russell and Sam Jones then retired. There would be no more miracles for the Celtics, as they struggled to a 34–48 mark in 1969–70. They missed the playoffs for the first time since 1949–50. Though they improved the following year, it wasn't enough to get into the playoffs.

30

Before the 1970–71 season, the NBA welcomed three new teams. It also split into two conferences—Eastern and Western—with two divisions apiece. Boston was now in the Eastern Conference's Atlantic Division. Tom Heinsohn became coach. The team added rookie center Dave Cowens. Boston won the Eastern Conference the following year and won 68 games in 1972–73, tying the all-time NBA record. But both times, it lost in the conference finals. Players such as rebounding specialist Paul Silas and high-scoring, durable guard Jo Jo White (who played a team-record 488 consecutive games) joined Cowens. The Celtics won NBA titles in 1974 and 1976.

Injuries and personnel issues haunted the 1977–78 season. Boston's 32–50 record was the worst since 1949–50. Heinsohn was fired midseason and replaced by Satch Sanders. The other former player didn't do any better. Sanders was gone by early the next season as the once-proud Celtics stumbled to a 29–53 finish.

Guard **JO JO WHITE** was a consistent force on the court for a decade in Boston.

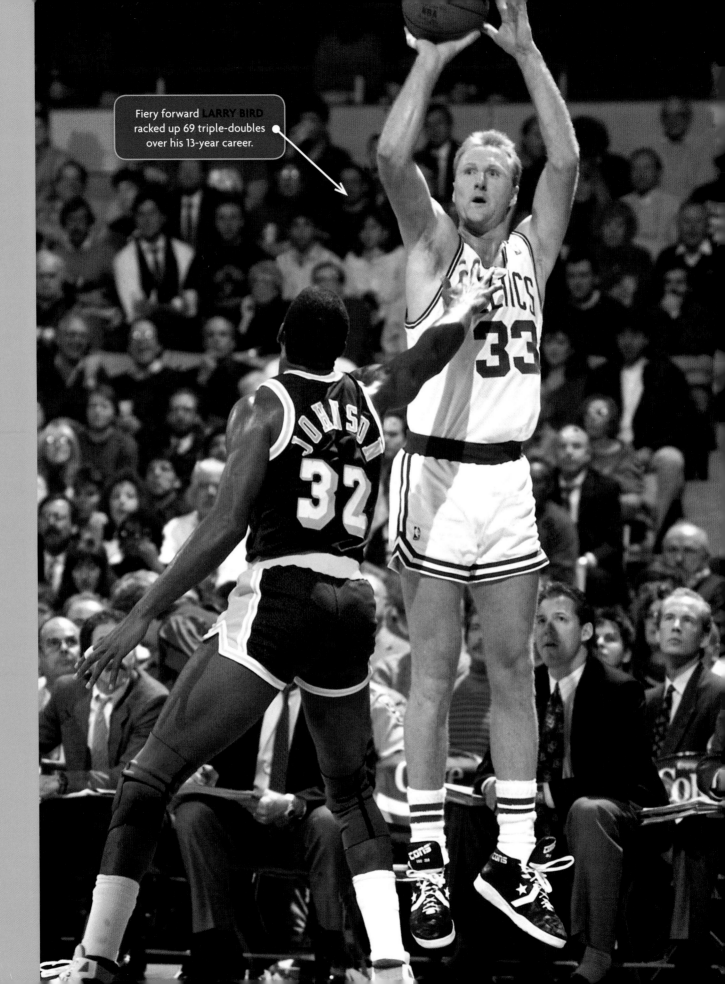

Fiery forward **LARRY BIRD** racked up 69 triple-doubles over his 13-year career.

BIRD TAKES A
BRIEF FLIGHT

f the Russell-Chamberlain rivalry is the NBA's most storied, a close second is that of another Celtics player. Forward Larry Bird and point guard Earvin "Magic" Johnson of the Lakers entered the league in

34

THE DUEL

GAME 7, EASTERN CONFERENCE SEMIFINALS, BOSTON VS. ATLANTA, MAY 22, 1988

Many people call this game the greatest individual duel in NBA playoff history. Boston led 84–82 after the third quarter. Atlanta's star forward Dominque Wilkins already had 31 points, while Larry Bird had just 14. At the start of the fourth quarter, Wilkins remembered, "Bird's eyes got like *this big*.... That's where the great shootout began." The two men matched each other shot for shot. Bird scored 20 points, Wilkins 16. Boston won 118–116 to capture the series. Hawks center Cliff Levingston said, "It was almost like a game of HORSE.... This was basically full court one-on-one, with a few guys out there to pass the ball and get out of the way."

"IT WAS ALMOST LIKE A GAME OF HORSE.... THIS WAS BASICALLY FULL COURT ONE-ON-ONE, WITH A FEW GUYS OUT THERE TO PASS THE BALL AND GET OUT OF THE WAY."

1979–80. Bird showcased his all-around greatness as a rookie. He scored 21.3 points, hauled down more than 10 rebounds, and dished out nearly 5 assists per game. With other players such as forward Cedric "Cornbread" Maxwell and shifty guard Nate Archibald, Boston soared to a 61–21 mark in 1979–80. That was a 32-game improvement in a single season. The team did even better the following season. It won 62 games and took the NBA title. The Celtics continued at a high level the following two seasons, though they didn't reach the NBA Finals. They went all the way in 1984 in an epic Finals matchup with Johnson's Lakers. Between two Lakers championships in 1985 and 1987, Boston defeated the Houston Rockets in the NBA Finals in 1986. Bird was not alone during this run of success. Center Robert Parish dominated the middle. Power forward/center Kevin McHale became almost unstoppable down low, first as the sixth man and later as a starter.

Boston remained successful for several more seasons. But it couldn't reach the NBA Finals. Bird's bad back made him retire before the 1992–93 season. The Celtics still made the playoffs that year. Then the bottom dropped out. The team had losing records for the next eight seasons. It made the playoffs just once. The worst was 1996–97, when Boston won just 15 games.

THE BIG THREE

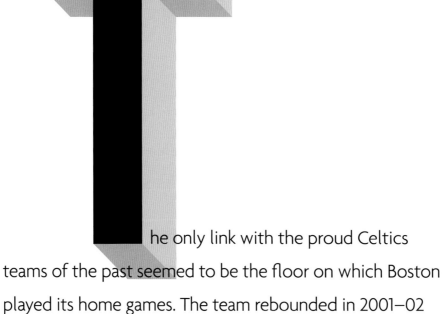

The only link with the proud Celtics teams of the past seemed to be the floor on which Boston played its home games. The team rebounded in 2001–02 behind forward/guard Paul Pierce and forward Antoine Walker. The two averaged nearly 50 points between them. Boston advanced to the Eastern Conference finals

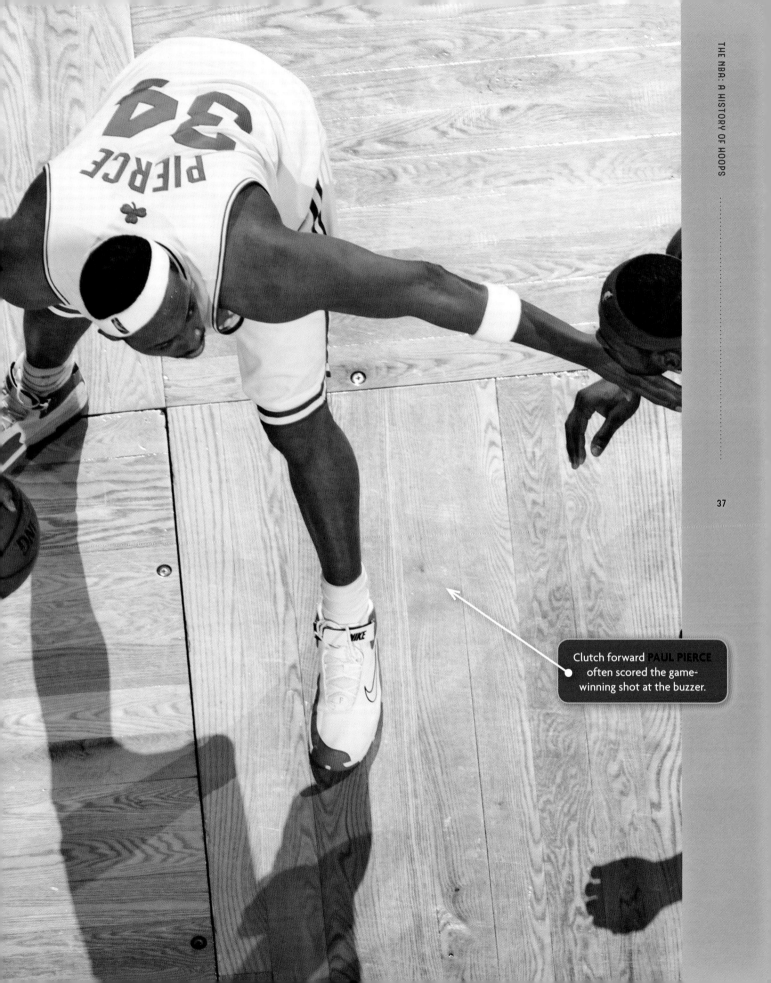

Clutch forward **PAUL PIERCE** often scored the game-winning shot at the buzzer.

With **KEVIN GARNETT'S** help, the Celtics returned to championship form in 2008.

> "I TOLD OUR GUYS AFTER THE GAME I COULDN'T HAVE BEEN PROUDER OF THIS GROUP."

before losing. The Celtics made the playoffs the following three years. Then they faltered and posted losing records in 2005–06 and 2006–07. Canny trades brought prolific shooting guard Ray Allen and dynamic center Kevin Garnett to Boston the following season. The newcomers and Pierce were immediately christened the "Big Three." Point guard Rajon Rondo brought stability to the backcourt. The Celtics soared to a 66–16 mark and beat Los Angeles for their 17th NBA title. They lost in the conference semifinals the following season. Then they pushed the Lakers to Game 7 in the 2009–10 NBA Finals before losing 83–79. "I told our guys after the game I couldn't have been prouder of this group," coach Doc Rivers said.

39

Defensive specialist **RAJON RONDO** led the league in steals (189) in 2009–10.

40

THE FLOOR SHOW ENDS

LEGENDS OF THE HARDWOOD

In 1946, owner Walter Brown wanted a new floor for his new team. Because of a lumber shortage after World War II, the Boston Lumber Company had to use pieces of scrap wood to build it. Workers placed the scraps together in an alternating pattern called a parquet that became the most distinctive playing surface in the NBA. Each of the 247 pieces measured 5'x5'x1.5". Team employees needed several hours to assemble the floor, using nearly 1,000 heavy bolts. It was finally replaced in 1999. Team officials cut it into small pieces. They sold the pieces to eager Boston fans who wanted a souvenir of the team's glory days.

he Celtics advanced to the
conference semifinals the following year and
conference finals in 2011–12. But Boston had just a 41–
40 mark and a first-round playoff exit in 2012–13. Under
new coach Brad Stevens, the team struggled to a 25–57
mark in 2013–14. It was just 20–31 in mid-February of
the following season. Then Boston traded for

42

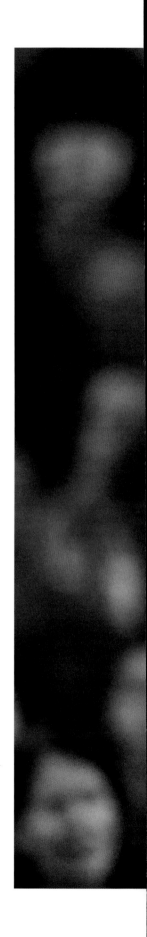

Hardworking guard **AVERY BRADLEY** developed into a reliable defender and scorer.

5-foot-9 ballhawking guard Isaiah Thomas. "Isaiah is a dynamic offensive player whose scoring and playmaking abilities add to an already well-rounded backcourt," said Celtics president of basketball operations Danny Ainge. "We are excited to welcome Isaiah to the Celtics family." Thomas justified Ainge's optimism. He averaged 19 points a game off the bench and sparked Boston to a berth. Despite losing in the first round, the Celtics featured one of the league's best young guard combinations. Shooting guard Avery Bradley and point guard Marcus Smart made good

Tough center **AL HORFORD** boosted Boston on both sides of the court.

MARCUS SMART energized the team with his hustle and passion for the game.

> "I'VE SEEN 13 TEAMS NOW AND THIS IS AS GOOD AN ENERGY—POSITIVE ENERGY AND TEAMWORK AS WE'VE HAD.... THESE GUYS ARE FIRED UP TO BE CELTICS; THEY ARE GLAD TO BE HERE. THEY'LL DO ANYTHING FOR THE TEAM."

on their first-round pick predictions. Boston went 48–34 in 2015–16. It was the team's best mark in five years. But Atlanta beat the Celtics in the first round of the playoffs, four games to two.

In his second year as a starter, Thomas led the Celtics to the top of the Eastern Conference in 2016–17. He set a team record by scoring 20 or more points in 43 straight games. He was also named to the All-NBA second team. After winning two closely fought series in the playoffs, the Celtics lost Thomas for most of the conference finals against Cleveland. Boston managed just one win against the overpowering Cavaliers.

With Boston's young team continually gaining valuable experience and a treasure chest full of extra draft picks in upcoming years, Celtics fans had reason for hope. As team owner Wyc Grousbeck noted, "I've seen 13 teams now and this is as good an energy—positive energy and teamwork as we've had.... These guys are fired up to be Celtics; they are glad to be here. They'll do anything for the team." Perhaps "anything" would look like an 18th championship banner hanging in the rafters of TD Garden.

SELECTED BIBLIOGRAPHY

Ballard, Chris. *The Art of a Beautiful Game: The Thinking Fan's Tour of the NBA*. New York: Simon & Schuster, 2010.

Freedman, Lew. *Dynasty: Auerbach, Cousy, Havlicek, Russell, and the Rise of the Boston Celtics*. Guilford, Conn.: Lyons Press, 2011.

Hubbard, Donald. *"Then Russell Said to Bird...": The Greatest Celtics Stories Ever Told*. Chicago: Triumph Books, 2013.

Hubbard, Jan, ed. *The Official NBA Basketball Encyclopedia*. 3rd edition. New York: Doubleday, 2000.

NBA.com. "Boston Celtics." http://www.nba.com/celtics/.

Sports Illustrated. *Sports Illustrated Basketball's Greatest*. New York: Sports Illustrated, 2014.

WEBSITES

CLUB GREEN KIDS

http://www.nba.com/celtics/clubgreen/clubgreen_kids.html

This official kids club website of the Boston Celtics features games, quizzes, pages to color, team history, news, and more.

JR. NBA

http://jr.nba.com/

This kids site has games, videos, game results, team and player information, statistics, and more.

Note: Every effort has been made to ensure that any websites listed above were active at the time of publication. However, because of the nature of the Internet, it is impossible to guarantee that these sites will remain active indefinitely or that their contents will not be altered.

INDEX